For Becky and Lenny

— NW

For Kevin, always

— ZS

Tundra Books, an imprint of Tundra Book Group, a division of Penguin Random House
of Canada Limited

Library and Archives Canada Cataloguing in Publication

Title: How to teach your cat a trick / Nicola Winstanley ; illustrated by Zoe Si.
Names: Winstanley, Nicola, author. | Si, Zoe, illustrator.
Identifiers: Canadiana (print) 20210351993 | Canadiana (ebook) 20210352019 |
ISBN 9780735270619 (hardcover) | ISBN 9780735270626 (EPUB)
Classification: LCC PS8645.I57278 H698 2022 | DDC jC813/.6—dc23

Published simultaneously in the United States of America by Tundra Books of
Northern New York, an imprint of Tundra Book Group, a division of Penguin Random
House of Canada Limited

Library of Congress Control Number: 2021949254

Edited by Samantha Swenson
Designed by John Martz and Sophie Paas-Lang
The artwork in this book was created digitally in Procreate.
The text was set in Century Std Book and Futura Std Extra Bold.

Printed in China

www.penguinrandomhouse.ca

1 2 3 4 5   26 25 24 23 22

Penguin
Random House
TUNDRA BOOKS

How to Teach Your Cat a Trick

IN FIVE EASY STEPS

TO SALTCHEESE & BAJI !

Nicola Winstanley

tundra

Zoe Si

Does your cat just lie around
all day and ignore you?

You need . . .

How to Teach Your Cat a Trick in Five Easy Steps

Cats are smarter than you think.
They can learn all kinds of new
things! Let's begin.

STEP ONE

Assess what your cat can do already.
Can your cat sit?

That's not sitting.

Hmm. Let's try something else.
Can he high-five? Jump? Circle?

Sigh. Can he . . . roll over?

Well done! Can he stay?

This might be harder than I thought.
Let's just move on to step two.

STEP TWO

Decide on a trick and get some
treats ready.

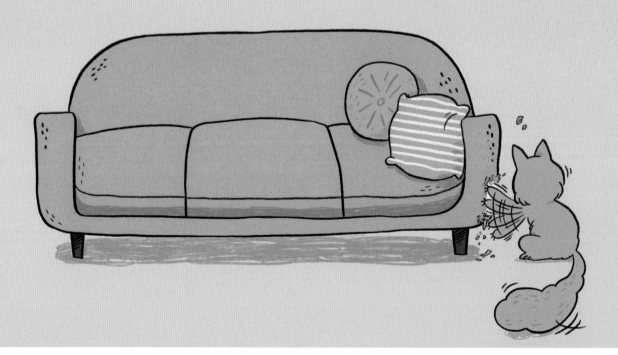

CAT treats.

OH!

We should start with an easy trick.

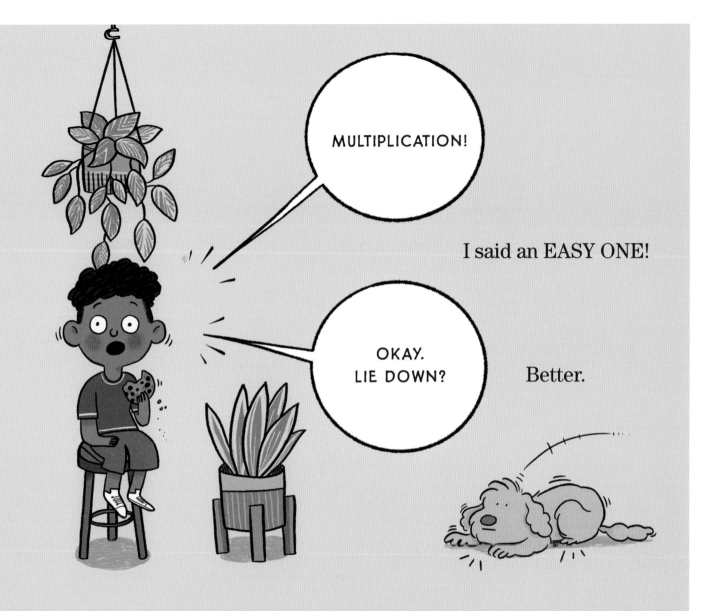

STEP THREE
Hold the treat in your hand and ask your
cat to lie down.

STEP FOUR
Repeat step three.

STEP SIX

Catch your cat. Quick!

Fine.

NEW STEP TWO
Find an area with no distractions.

STEP THREE
Hold a treat in your hand
and ask your cat to lie —

Fine, you win.

How to Teach Your Cat a Trick
in One Easy Step

STEP ONE
Lie down.
Your cat will lie on top of you.